DILYS PRICE

NORMAN
PRICE

BELLA
LASAGNE

JAMES

SARAH

MEET ALL THESE FRIENDS IN BUZZ BOOKS:

Thomas the Tank Engine
Fireman Sam
Bugs Bunny
Looney Tunes
Tiny Toon Adventures
Police Academy
Toucan 'Tecs
Flintstones
Jetsons
Joshua Jones

First published by Buzz Books,
an imprint of Reed International Books Ltd
Michelin House, 81 Fulham Road, London SW3 6RB

LONDON MELBOURNE AUCKLAND

Fireman Sam © copyright 1985 Prism Art & Design Ltd
Text © copyright 1992 William HeinemannLtd
Illustrations © copyright 1992 William Heinemann Ltd
Based on the animation series produced by Bumper Films
for S4C/Channel 4 Wales and Prism Art & Design Ltd.
Original idea by Dave Gingell and Dave Jones,
assisted by Mike Young. Characters created by Rob Lee.
All rights reserved.

ISBN 1 85591 213 9

Printed and bound in the UK by BPCC Hazell Books Ltd

NORMAN AND THE
RUNAWAY COW

Story by Rob Lee
Illustrations by The County Studio

Fireman Sam was driving through the winding country lanes of Pontypandy. Elvis needed cabbage and potatoes to cook supper at the station.

"I'll ask Trevor for some fresh vegetables from his allotment," said Fireman Sam.

He drove along Pandy Lane until he arrived at Trevor's allotment.

As he climbed down from Jupiter, Fireman Sam saw Trevor racing around the allotment waving his hands above his head and shouting, "Shoo! Shoo!"

"Great fires of London!" cried Fireman Sam.
"What on earth are you doing, Trevor?"

"I'm trying to frighten the crows away!"
moaned Trevor. "They're eating all my
vegetables!"

"What you need is a scarecrow," said
Fireman Sam.

8

"I've tried that," said Trevor. "The crows used it as a perch!"

Trevor took his spade and began digging up potatoes. "I can give you a nice sack of spuds," said Trevor, "but I'm afraid my cabbages are ruined!"

"Perhaps you could make me something to scare the birds away," said Trevor as Fireman Sam got ready to leave.

Fireman Sam went to Dilys Price's shop to buy a cabbage.

"What's the matter, Dilys?" he asked, pointing to the cotton wool in her ears.

"Pardon?" said Dilys loudly.

Suddenly Sam heard an awful screeching noise. He clapped his hands over his ears.

Dilys smiled and removed the cotton wool. "My darling Norman is practising the violin. I tell him practice makes perfect, but I'm afraid he still has far to go."

"I'll say!" chuckled Fireman Sam as he picked a large cabbage.

Suddenly, beautiful violin music came wafting through the shop.

"That's much better!" said Fireman Sam.

"Ah!" cooed Dilys. "He's a little genius!"

Fireman Sam walked in carrying the cabbage and potatoes.

"Great!" cried Elvis. "That's just what I need for my goulash with sour cabbage!"

"A simple roast dinner would do!" groaned Station Officer Steele.

By now, Norman was out at Pandy Farm carrying a lasso.

"Two-gun Norman Price is gonna rustle some steers," drawled Norman.

But when Norman saw Farmer Jones' cow, Daisy, he had second thoughts.

"Er, that's a big s-steer!" he said.

"Time to make tracks," gulped Norman as he scuttled away.

Unfortunately, when Norman ran out of the field, he forgot to close the gate behind him and Daisy wandered out.

17

At that moment, Firefighter Penny Morris was on her way to Pontypandy Fire Station in Venus. As she came round a bend, she almost collided with Daisy who was crossing the road.

"Watch out!" cried Penny as she beeped the horn before swerving across the road. Startled, Daisy gave a loud "Moo!" and ran off as fast as she could.

"I'd better get after her!" said Penny, climbing out of Venus.

Daisy lumbered across the wet fields until
she lost her footing and slithered down the
bank of a muddy stream. Daisy tried to
climb out of the stream, but the more she
struggled the more she became stuck.

20

"I'd better get help!" said Penny, when she saw what had happened. She hurried back to Venus to call the station. "Venus one to Pontypandy Fire Station, I need help to rescue a stranded cow, over," said Penny.

"Help on the way, over!" replied Station Officer Steele.

Fireman Sam and the crew sprang into action. Penny had just unloaded the winch and pulley from the rescue tender when they arrived.

"Let's get to work," said Station Officer Steele as Daisy mooed loudly.

"I'll use that tree as a hoist," said Penny.

22

As she attached the cable to the tree, Sam
and Elvis waded into the stream to fasten
the sling round Daisy. Frightened, Daisy
mooed louder. Bit by bit, they winched her
out of the mud.

"Easy, easy..." said Station Officer Steele.
"That's it! Well done!"

23

"Good old Daisy!" said Penny. "Rescued, and without a scratch!"

"Plenty of mud, though," said Elvis.

"We'll soon get rid of that!" chuckled Fireman Sam, as he made for Jupiter. "All she needs is a little shower!"

As Fireman Sam gently hosed the mud from Daisy, she mooed with delight.

J 999

"I wonder how Daisy managed to get out of her field?" asked Penny.

Just then, Norman appeared from behind a bush.

"Stick 'em up, you critters!"

"Something tells me a certain little outlaw had something to do with it!" said Fireman Sam.

"If this was your fault Norman, the sheriff is going to take you back to town and toss you in the jailhouse!" drawled Fireman Sam.

"I didn't t-touch Daisy, honest!" replied Norman.

"You didn't close the gate behind you either," said Penny sternly.

Fireman Sam thought for a moment, then said, "I think it's time you had some more violin practice, Norman!"

Later, Fireman Sam and Trevor were sitting outside Trevor's allotment shed.

"I don't think you'll have a problem with the crows now," chuckled Fireman Sam as he handed a piece of cotton wool to Trevor. "Off you go, Norman!" he called.

A screeching, wailing noise split the air as Norman marched up and down playing his violin.

Trevor watched the crows scatter, then looked across at Fireman Sam. "I almost feel sorry for the birds," he chuckled.

FIREMAN SAM

STATION OFFICER
STEELE

TREVOR EVANS

ELVIS
CRIDLINGTON

PENNY MORRIS